T H E

Creature

SADDLEBACK
EDUCATIONAL PUBLISHING

T H E   H E I G H T S

Blizzard	Ransom
Camp	River
Crash	Sail
Creature	Score
Dam	Shelter
Dive	Swamp
Heist	Treasure
Jump	Tsunami
Mudslide	Twister
Neptune	Wild

Original text by Ed Hansen
Adapted by Mary Kate Doman

SADDLEBACK
EDUCATIONAL PUBLISHING
www.sdlback.com

ISBN-13: 978-1-62250-050-5
ISBN-10: 1-62250-050-4
eBook: 978-1-61247-708-4

Printed in the U.S.A.

21 20 19 18 17   5 6 7 8 9

Chapter 1

Tate Moore was a nature camp leader. He was leading eight teenage boys on a camping trip at Bear Lake. Most of the teens had never camped before. But they'd done a great job hiking and setting up the campsite.

Everyone had a task. Some campers set up tents. A few others helped make a big campfire. Two boys even cooked dinner.

After dinner everyone told scary stories. It had been a long day. Tate and all the campers fell asleep after they put out the campfire.

It was after two in the morning when Tate left his tent to use the bathroom. He was only twenty yards away. Then something hit him from behind. Tate fell to the ground. He screamed. But no one heard him. His mouth was full of dirt. Whatever attacked him was big and strong.

Tate Moore struggled. But it was no use. He was carried deep into the woods.

Sunrise was at six thirty. Even though it was early, the teens got up. They were excited. Today there would be hiking, rock climbing, and fishing.

But the teens knew something was wrong. Tate's tent was empty. They called his name. But there was no answer. They searched the area. Then one of the campers saw Tate's flashlight. There was some blood next to it. The boys got Tate's cell phone. They called the police. The police came quickly. So did two forest rangers.

Officers searched the campsite. They found nothing besides the flashlight and blood. Police and forest rangers continued their search for two days. Nothing turned up. Someone—or something—had made off with Tate Moore. And no one knew who—or *what*—it was!

Chapter 2

Two weeks had passed since Tate
Moore disappeared. The police
were puzzled. They'd ruled out a
bear. Bears didn't drag their prey.
They killed prey right where it
fell. Mountain lions were extinct in
these parts. And there were no other
animals in the area that could attack
a grown man.

The next day the phone rang at the Rockdale Heights Police Department. Officer Pitt picked it up.

"This is Liv Cutts," a woman said. "My husband, Sam, is missing."

"How long has he been gone?" asked Officer Pitt.

"Since yesterday," Liv replied. "He went fishing at Bear Lake. But he never came home."

Officer Pitt froze. He knew about Tate Moore. The officer told Liv he would begin searching for Sam. Then he went to talk to the chief.

"We have another missing person at Bear Lake," Officer Pitt said.

"Oh no! What happened?" Chief Vega asked.

"Sam Cutts is missing," the officer

said. "His wife just called. He went fishing yesterday and never came home."

"Let's hope it's not the same thing that got Tate Moore. It will be a big problem if it is," Chief Vega said.

The chief called Max Winn. Max was the head forest ranger. And he'd led the search for Tate.

The two men decided to search the lake for Sam. Other officers and rangers helped too. Everyone got to the lake before noon. Sam Cutts's truck was parked next to a trail. The trail led to the lake.

There was a lot of ground to cover. The twelve-member search party split up. The two groups would meet back at Sam's truck. Max Winn led a group into the woods. Chief Vega led a group around the lake.

Chief Vega and his men found nothing. Walking back to the truck, they ran into Max.

"We didn't find anything. How about you guys?" the chief asked.

Max nodded. He took out his phone. He showed the chief a photo. The chief winced. Max asked everyone to follow him. They walked a mile.

Chief Vega stared down at a ripped shirt. Beside it was a bloody human hand! It had been torn off at the wrist. The bones were crushed. The photo was awful. This was worse.

"There's blood everywhere," Max said. "But there's no body. Whatever did this is long gone."

Chapter 3

Lilia Silva arrived at a popular running trail on the far side of Bear Lake. She was meeting her teammate Macy Kent for a ten-mile run. Both girls were stars on the Rockdale Heights track team.

The girls would jog together for the first eight miles. Then, with two miles to go, they would pick up the pace. Each would go as fast as she could. Lilia usually ran a few yards ahead of Macy.

After seven miles, the girls were deep in the forest. Neither one noticed the large creature in the woods. It quietly ran alongside them. Its red eyes stared at them. At mile eight, Lilia ran past Macy.

"See you at the finish line," Lilia yelled.

Macy watched Lilia disappear down the trail.

Lilia was forty yards ahead when she thought she heard a scream. She stopped and listened. She heard it again. It was Macy. Lilia ran back up the trail as fast as she could.

Something was headed into the woods. And it had Macy. Lilia

screamed, "*Stop!*" Then she picked up a big branch. She continued screaming. She banged the branch against the trees. All the noise scared the creature. It dropped Macy and ran into the woods.

"Macy! Are you all right?" Lilia yelled.

Macy didn't answer. She was in shock. Blood was running down her forehead. And her arm was badly cut. Lilia carried Macy down the trail on her back.

When Lilia reached the main road, she flagged down a car. A half hour later, Macy was in the emergency room.

Lilia called Macy's mom. Then she called her dad, Rafael Silva. She told them about the attack. Both hurried to the hospital.

Before arriving, Rafael called Chief Vega. He told him about the attack. The chief was stunned. He'd just been at Bear Lake! The bloody hand was still fresh in his mind.

"Rafael, I need to talk to Lilia," the chief said. "I'll meet you at the hospital."

The men met outside the waiting room.

"Thanks for coming," Rafael said. "But I could have brought Lilia to your office."

"I know. But something very strange is happening around Bear Lake," Chief Vega said. "A few weeks ago a guide went missing. Today we got a call about a missing fisherman. And from what we found, there is no way he's alive. We have no idea what's doing this. I hope Lilia can help us."

"It's so dangerous. You should close the lake," Rafael said.

Just then Mrs. Kent ran past them. She went into the waiting room. And she ran over to Lilia and gave her a big hug.

"Macy is going to be okay. And it's all because of you. You saved her life," Mrs. Kent said.

"I'm so glad," Lilia said. "I knew I needed to get Macy out of there. I know she would have done the same for me."

Then Lilia noticed her dad and Chief Vega. Rafael walked over and gave his daughter a hug.

"Hey, Lil," Rafael said. "Are you okay?"

"Yes," Lilia replied. "Macy is too."

"That's very good to hear," Chief Vega said. "But I need to ask you a few questions. What happened, Lilia?"

"Everything happened so fast. I don't remember much. That creature … Whatever it was, it was fast and scared," Lilia said.

"Think hard," said Chief Vega. "What exactly did you see? You said 'it'—not 'who.' Was it an animal?"

"It was some kind of creature. I don't know what it was," Lilia said. "But it walked on all fours. And it had a very long tail!"

Chapter 4

The police tried to keep the attacks
a secret. They didn't want people to
panic. But it was too late. Someone
leaked the story to the press. The
headline in the local paper read:

MYSTERIOUS CREATURE
ATTACKS THIRD VICTIM

The story made the national
news. Macy didn't remember a thing.
So reporters from all over wanted

to interview Lilia. She was the only person who'd seen the beast. Rafael and Ana tried to keep the press away.

Professor Marks was a biologist. He saw the story about the attacks. He couldn't believe it. He called the Rockdale Heights Police Department. And he asked to speak with the chief.

"Hello, Chief, I'm Professor Marks. I was a researcher with the university field office. The office was in the woods near Bear Lake. A tornado destroyed it last year," he said.

"Oh yes," said Chief Vega. "I remember it. That huge storm came through. That office was totaled. Gone."

"I think I know what's causing the attacks. I can't talk about it over the phone. Will you be around later today?" Professor Marks asked.

They set up a meeting. Chief Vega called Max Winn and Rafael Silva. He thought they needed to hear what the professor knew too. The four men met in Chief Vega's office.

"I worked at the field office for six years," Professor Marks said. "I worked on a top-secret project. Our goal was to help endangered animals. While doing that, we created a new animal."

The men looked at each other. None of them knew what to say.

"You know that mountain lions are endangered. They are extinct on the East Coast. That's why we decided to make a new kind of lion," the professor said. "So we mixed in some black bear DNA. We bred them in our lab."

"You made a new animal?" Rafael asked. "I didn't even know that was possible."

"Yes. It was a cross between a mountain lion and a bear. We called it a *bion*," said the professor. "It was amazing! Nothing like this had ever been done before. We had a bion cub that was over fifty pounds.

"We were about to tell the press. But then the tornado hit. The field office was destroyed. The building collapsed. Everything was gone. We thought the bion cub died in the wreckage," Professor Marks said. "But after hearing about the creature at Bear Lake, I'm not so sure."

"If the bion is still alive, how big would it be?" Max Winn asked.

"I guess it's around three hundred fifty pounds," replied the professor.

Chief Vega stared at him. He was angry.

"Why did you just assume the bion cub was dead? Why didn't you tell anyone about this?" the chief asked. "At least two people are dead because of you!"

"I'm sorry," Professor Marks said. "I made a big mistake."

"Yes, you did," Max Winn said. "But how do we kill this thing before it kills someone else?"

"You can't kill it!" yelled Professor Marks. "It's an amazing new animal! We need to catch it. We need to study it. It could save many endangered animals."

"How do we catch this bion?" Rafael asked.

"It won't be easy, Mr. Silva," the professor replied. "But I have a plan."

Chapter 5

Van Suggs followed the Bear Lake
attacks closely. He was a hunter. He
knew the woods around Bear Lake
better than anyone.

Van decided to hunt down the
creature. He loaded up his truck
with camping gear. He also brought
three rifles and a lot of bullets.
Right before he left, Van called his
friend Nick.

"Hi, Nick," Van said. "I'm heading over to Bear Lake. I know the road is closed. But I'm going anyway. I'm going to hunt down that mystery beast. How about you come up in a few days? You can help me search."

"Sure thing," Nick said. "I'd like to get a look at that creature myself. I'll be there in a couple days. Good luck."

"Sounds good, Nick," said Van.

Van got up to Bear Lake and set up camp. Then he loaded his rifles.

The next day Van searched the woods. He found nothing. That night he set a trap for the creature. Van tied some fresh meat to a tree. Then he hid.

Van Suggs didn't make it till morning. The animal he was hunting attacked him from behind. The hunter had become the hunted.

Two days later Nick went to the lake. He knew something was wrong. Van's rifle and hat were on the ground. He screamed when he saw Van's tent. It was ripped to shreds. Pieces of it were everywhere. And there was blood. Lots of blood.

Nick was very upset. He knew his friend was dead.

Chapter 6

The professor gave the chief,
Max, and Rafael a quick lesson on
mountain lions. The missing bion
was acting just like a full-grown
lion.

"Lions have great eyesight,
hearing, and sense of smell. They
are perfect hunters," said Professor
Marks. "Their prey never sees them
until after they attack. And when

they strike, it's almost always from behind."

"Why haven't we found any of its victims?" asked Max.

"Lions don't eat their prey right where they find them. They carry it to where they feel safe. Then they eat it," the professor said.

"How do we catch this thing?" Chief Vega asked.

"We know it has caught prey by Bear Lake. We need to put a big trap up there. We can fill it with fresh meat. The bion may try to get the meat. Then we can catch it. And we can fly it out. The zoo is dropping off the trap at the lake now," Professor Marks said.

"All access to Bear Lake is closed," the chief said. "We need to meet them up there."

"There's one more thing," the professor said. "Someone needs to watch the cage at all times. We can't risk the bion getting out. It's a very smart animal. If it escapes, it will remember the trap. Then it won't go near a cage again."

Everyone said they'd help guard the trap.

"All the attacks have happened near the lake. I think the best place to hide is in a boat on the lake," Rafael said. "I have a boat we can use. It will be comfortable and keep us safe from the bion."

"Perfect," said Chief Vega. "Rafael, get the boat. We'll all meet at Bear Lake in two hours."

The cage was at the lake when the men got there. It was eight by fourteen feet. There was a big hook to hold the meat. A cable ran from the hook to the front door. It was open now. But if something grabbed the meat, the door would slam shut. It was the perfect trap.

It was dark by the time they set everything up. Professor Marks and Max Winn took the first watch. They went out to Rafael's boat to keep an eye on the cage.

It was cold and dark on the lake. Professor Marks looked into the darkness. He knew the bion was out there. But he couldn't see it.

Around three in the morning, the men woke to a loud *bang*! The metal door on the cage had slammed shut.

Chapter 7

The professor couldn't wait to see the bion. He tried to get Max to go ashore with him.

"No way!" Max said. "It's too dark. There are lots of other animals in the woods. And if the bion isn't in that cage, he's still out there. Loose. We don't want to be walking around the lake now."

"I guess you're right," Professor Marks replied.

The two men got to the cage as soon as it was light. They couldn't believe their eyes. A black bear was inside!

"How are we going to get it out?" the professor asked.

"Very carefully," Max replied.

They were very upset. They thought that they'd caught the bion. Max called his forest rangers to help with the bear. Then he called Chief Vega with the news.

"That's too bad," the chief said.

"Some rangers are coming over with a ladder. They can help us open the cage. We'll let the bear out," said Max.

Max and his team let the bear out. They used the ladder to climb on top of the cage. Then they opened the door. The bear ran into the woods. After the bear was gone, they set the trap again. They watched the cage late into the day.

Later that afternoon Rafael and Antonio were on duty. They took the boat out on the lake. Rafael and Antonio looked at the cage. Nothing seemed to be happening. But then they saw something moving on shore. Rafael tried to get a better view.

"What's that, Dad?" Antonio asked.

"It's just a fox," Rafael replied. "I bet it smelled the meat. I hope it doesn't set off the trap."

But the fox ran inside the open cage and grabbed the meat. Once again the door slammed shut.

"We have to get it out of there," said Rafael. "We need to reset the trap. We can't catch the bion if we don't."

They took the boat to shore. Rafael told Antonio to stay in the boat while he set the fox free.

A pair of red eyes watched Rafael from the woods. Rafael freed the fox. Then the bion ran straight for him. Antonio saw the whole thing.

"Dad! Bion!" Antonio yelled. "Run!"

Rafael knew that his only hope was the water. He ran to the lake.

Then he dived in. The bion was
right behind him. Rafael came up
twenty-five yards from shore. The
bion didn't get in the water. It stayed
on shore, pacing. Antonio swore the
bion looked disappointed.

Chapter 8

"Do you think the bion will come
back later?" Antonio asked. "It's
going to get dark soon."

"It may," replied Rafael. "We know
it's hungry. And it doesn't know we're
out here on the lake. But don't worry.
We're not leaving this boat until we're
sure the bion is in the trap!"

Soon the quiet evening was
cut short. First there was a loud

slamming sound. Then a loud growl cut through the air. Rafael and Antonio sat up. They looked toward shore. It was still light enough to see. The plan worked. The bion was trapped in the cage!

Rafael and Antonio went ashore. From a safe distance, they looked at the bion. No one had ever seen a full-grown bion before. It was over nine feet long. It had a huge head and paws. The bion was the coolest thing they had ever seen. And *very* scary.

Rafael called Chief Vega and told him the good news.

"That's great!" the chief said. "I'll tell the professor. Then I'll radio the chopper to come at dawn. It's too dangerous to pick up the cage at night. The chopper will airlift the cage to the zoo."

Professor Marks and Chief Vega were at Bear Lake in less than an hour. The chief went right to work. The professor couldn't take his eyes off the cage.

"Well, professor," said Rafael, "you got your wish."

"Yes, I did," the professor said. "Thank you so much! This bion is more than I ever imagined. It's bigger. It's stronger. And it's more beautiful than I ever hope for. I think this is the beginning of a new species."

"It *is* a beautiful animal. But also remember how deadly it is," Chief

Vega said. "Your bion has killed at least three people."

"I know that. I'm very sorry," the professor said. "It will never hurt anyone again. I'm taking it to a new lab. We'll study it. Then we'll use what we learn to help save animals all over the world."

A team of police and rangers spent the night. Everyone was amazed. The creature was beautiful. But everyone was afraid. The creature was also really angry. It did not like the cage.

At dawn the chopper arrived at the lake. Everyone helped hook the cage to the bottom of the chopper. Professor Marks and Chief Vega climbed aboard.

Rafael and Antonio watched the chopper fly out of sight. The bion's cage hung underneath.

"Dad, that bion seemed smarter than a bear. It seemed smarter than a mountain lion too," mused Antonio. "Do you think the professor used other DNA?"

"You're right, son," said Rafael. "I'm not sure I believe the professor."

Chapter 9

The flight from Bear Lake to the airport should have been quick. But this time it was different.

The weight of the cage was too heavy. It was more than the chopper could handle.

After a few minutes in the air, the chopper had problems. The cage got stuck in a tall tree. The chopper jerked backward, then fell from the sky. It landed in a thick, dark part of the woods.

"Is everyone okay?" Chief Vega asked.

Both the professor and pilot answered. They were fine.

"Wait!" Professor Marks screamed. "Where's the cage?"

The three men carefully got out of the chopper. They saw the cage right away. It was lying on its side. It was damaged. The door was torn off. And it was empty. The bion was gone!

Everyone was in shock. No one said a word. Professor Marks was upset by the loss of his creation. Chief Vega knew a killer animal was loose. And the pilot thought it was his fault.

The three men started walking. They had a long way to go.

"Come on," said Chief Vega. "I don't want to be in the woods after dark with that creature around!"

They hurried through the woods as fast as they could. They listened for the bion. But they never heard its cries.

By noon they stumbled out of the woods. A police car drove by. It stopped when it saw three men standing in the road. The officer was shocked to find out one of them was Chief Vega.

"We've been looking for you all over, Chief," said the officer.

"Well, you found me now," the chief said. "We have to go back to

Bear Lake. We have to catch that bion again."

"That may be a problem, Chief," said Professor Marks.

"What do you mean?" asked the chief.

"I told you before that this bion was smart. It will never go near a cage again," the professor said. "We had one chance to catch it with that trap. And we blew it. From now on it'll be on its guard. Catching it again will be tough."

Chapter 10

Two months had passed. The escaped bion still had not been caught. Both Chief Vega and Max Winn had their best men on the job. They set traps all over the woods. Forest rangers put fresh meat in them every day. But there was no sign of the bion.

Everyone was disappointed. It seemed like the bion had outsmarted them. The mayor thought they were wasting money. A lot of people thought the bion died in the crash. And since it hadn't attacked anyone else, the mayor stopped the search.

They reopened the woods just in time for hunting season.

"We'll know soon if that thing is still alive," Max Winn said. "The woods are going to be filled with campers and hikers. Someone will see something."

"If it's alive, I just hope it doesn't start eating people again," said Chief Vega.

But hunting season came and went. There were no more bion attacks. Everyone agreed that it had died.

A year passed. Rafael thought it was safe to go to Bear Lake again. So he took Antonio on a weekend camping trip.

"This is so much better than the last time we were here," Antonio said.

"Yes, it is!" Rafael replied. "I really thought that bion was going to get me."

On the first night they hiked deep into the woods. Something strange caught Rafael's eye. The remains of a half-eaten deer lay in front of a dark cave. Next to the deer was a set of very large cat tracks.

Rafael and Antonio ran back to their campsite and packed up their gear. They didn't see the pair of red eyes watching them leave Bear Lake.